CW00400522

# Bad Omen

THE BROTHERHOOD OF BASTARDS
**PREQUEL**

# ALEX KING

We're twins, enemies, the kind of people with too many resources and just enough bad attitudes to ruin your day.

Neither of us knew it. It looked like privilege instead of a blood oath until it was too late to decline the invite. As the first born by minutes I was forced to take their corrupt throne.

He grew up a spare while I grew up a king.

He grew up thinking he was a bad omen, and I was some kind of lucky charm. So lucky that not even the untapped power could fix me. I was damaged goods and the ring on my finger wasn't any kind of Xanax.

Ambrose hated me before he could mutter the words and made my life hell to prove it.

Even taking Clover West from me.

He might have made life hell, but I was about to make his reality unbearable for stealing my queen.

# AUTHOR'S NOTE

Thank you so much for diving into this prequel... it may be short but it's powerful. Cassius McCall demanded to have a say, to have a voice, and denying him felt like a disservice to the series.

If you have read my prior work the same warning applies to this work. It is NOT a light read, it is not going to give you the warm-and-fuzzies. Instead think iron butterflies further south mixed with heavy triggers and all the secret society vibes.

Suicide, death of parents, secrets and lies, secret society/cult and more. This will be the lightest amount of words in this series so proceed with caution. The Brotherhood is coming...

*To the muse who requires only the most bad ass book boyfriends. This one's for you.*

# Chapter 1

## Clover

THE WEST WOMEN WERE CURSED.

They died young and beautiful, none lived past their thir-
ties, each dying a tragic death before they ever really started
living.

The daughters were the ones left behind, forced to care for
their broken-hearted fathers until they suffered the same stale
fate. Leaving us more broken than we started.

*Well, leaving* me *more broken than I started.*

I was the only daughter left. Last of the West family name,
the last reminder that my mother had existed at all, if only too
briefly.

I knew I was next even though I never felt sick. I had been

sheltered from harm and expected to treat life as fragilely as everyone treated me. After my mother died from that same genetic, heirloom curse, every worry transferred to me.

Suddenly, everything became calculating risks, assessing possible damage, and avoiding anything that could cut my life even shorter.

Until I resented the cage, I willingly put myself in and longed for the years I barely remembered anymore.

I wasn't always wrapped up in the harsh reminder that I was next.

Up until my mother died when I was ten, I was free. I could fall, I could have friends, I could take every risk without consequences. I barely remembered a time before my father's paranoia and fear kept him hostage.

This was just life now.

*Safe.*

Eventually, I convinced my dad to stop homeschooling me and let me go to the local public school—the infamous *Heritage High* as a freshman. That's where I found out how cruel the world is. I learned that most risks aren't worth taking, people are more than willing to cut you down, and vulnerability is a weakness they will use against you.

What they didn't know was that I was born to die and dying to live, and once you make peace with dying almost no one can tear you down.

Unless their name is *Ambrose McCall*.

He was more deadly than what was killing me, and neither had a cure.

Ambrose took every delight in making sure I flinched at his cruelty, but his relentless bullying and the pranks meant to break me only made me stronger.

I was starved and the freedom had fed the parts of me still

saying "*please, thank you*," and "*can I have some more of your bullshit?*" until they were satisfied. All those parts of me used to living so carefully were being snuffed out by the friction of the cruel world.

I wanted to kill every part of myself that was associated with weakness. So that was exactly what I did... I killed the Clover that had become the victim so that I could reinvent myself. I would turn into something they feared instead of attacked.

*Death could go fuck itself because I wasn't going to...*

My desire to live outweighed the truth of the curse my name held.

Heritage High felt like a privilege and a curse.

It wasn't a movie, there were no slow-motion struts through the halls, and popularity? Wasn't shit compared to being considered elite. And I wasn't *either* of those.

I was the homeschool freak that everyone considered a disease they didn't want to catch so I ate lunch alone after I pissed off the one person everyone took a knee for. One calculated risk I didn't account for.

*Ambrose McCall.*

He was elite, privileged, and sported a winning personality that only made you wonder what he was compensating for. I took every opportunity to avoid him until Cassius McCall, his twin brother, taught me how to stand up for myself.

My spine straightened when he was around, my shoulders pushed back, and my eyes clouded with hate every time we ended up in the same hallway. I was meek until Cassius showed me exactly how much power I had.

Ruining Ambrose's day and his disciples who helped him make me miserable became my favorite hobby. Lobbing insults back and forth became more of a hobby; it became a bad habit that neither one of us were willing to walk away from.

The hallway was littered with flyers, the senior kickback stamped all over each neon green sheet of paper stuck to the lockers and walls. It was hard to miss the one night everyone tried to destroy their futures.

Blowing off steam was almost required at the level Heritage High taught, it felt like an Ivy League College, yet we were just on the heels of freedom. Nothing about turning eighteen felt like freedom, it was just a reminder one more year had gone by and there still wasn't a cure for the kind of sick I was.

My alarm sounded off quietly, mostly a rough vibration with the pill emojis popping up on my screen. Slipping my routine medicine past my lips with my face almost inside my locker ashamed. Almost everyone was on something, vices wreaking havoc on their senses in order to survive high school.

There was never going to be a cure, a remission, there were only more drugs and more treatments in my future.

After all these years I thought I would have come to terms with my fate, but it only made me angrier. My time was running out.

Opening my locker, I stood there staring at the vast emptiness, my locker was void of anything but two textbooks and a small mirror hanging on the door. When you know your terminal, you try to leave no fingerprints behind so it's easier for people to imagine when you'll be gone.

The only impression I was leaving behind was being the only one brave enough to stand up to Ambrose when everyone else cowered.

"Don't hate me..." Cassius engulfed me from behind, his arms wrapping around my neck casually. "I can't make it this weekend..."

We were supposed to blow off the kickback and watch 90's movies until dawn rolled around. It was hard to hide the disappointment when I inhaled all the air my lungs would hold. "Seriously? You're gonna miss our marathon?"

Standing there still I soaked up his scent: a musky cologne hiding the fact that he didn't shower again and probably spent most of the night up smoking pot on his roof like he did every night.

Cassius was unapologetically himself. He was proud of his bad habits and had enough silent respect from people to not be bothered correcting any of them.

His arms resting on my shoulders loosened enough for his fingers to tickle my neck when he whispered into the shell of my ear. "I can be convinced to blow off dear old daddy, *Lover*."

I broke out in goosebumps when the nickname he only used came out as a hot breath teasing me.

Pushing my ass back I tried to shrug off his weight. "We are definitely not doing that. You know the rules."

The rules he constantly ignored to not ruin our friendship.

Cassius was gorgeous, the kind of gorgeous that felt effortless unlike his brother. Shaggy hair falling into his face, these blue eyes that felt illegal, cheekbones that took your breath away, and underneath the baggy clothes I had gotten mere glimpses of every muscle you wouldn't know he had. But I couldn't force myself to feel the way he obviously wanted me to.

We were best friends with no benefits. Not while Ambrose had occupied every spot of my heart still.

We might be enemies, but my entire body ached for him to fight with.

"Rules are meant to be broken, Lover. How long are we

going to pretend…" His voice trailed off instead of finishing his own question when he moved around me. Leaning into the lockers beside mine his eyes rolled down me like I was being hunted.

Playfully shoving my hand into his shoulder, he rocked backwards, stumbling to gain composure again. His relaxed expression suddenly turned cold and vicious when he muttered his words. "*Royalty* has arrived."

That was what we jokingly called them even though our town had rumors about royals, the brotherhood, the elite society no one knew actually existed. Rumors like everyone who had disappeared from this town was because of them.

It was an urban myth this town ate up like air, creating holidays and rituals just to appease them. Unlike the rest of the town, I opted to not care if they existed. I wasn't going to be a slave to their every word.

I could feel all of me winding up, tensing, even the features my face normally wore so casually. "You mean the *bastards*," I snapped at Cassius standing next to me.

Focusing all my attention on my books seems pointless when they demand your attention. I didn't have to look in their direction to know Ambrose was leading his cohorts down the hallway, flanking either side of him pretentiously like a bad joke. The worst part was how easily everyone would move out of their way.

Rolling my eyes at the thought I grabbed my textbook when my phone buzzed in my closed fist, pulling me from the thoughts I had been lost in front of my locker before the bell tolled through the halls. All around me, phones buzzed and chimed, the sound echoing throughout the Senior hallway. Everyone's heads dropped to their screens, soaking it up.

I didn't need to open the message to know it was going to

be *anonymous*. There were only three people who texted me: Cassius who stood next to me grilling his brother down, my dad who was working, and *anonymous*.

For the last few weeks, I had been the target of some kind of sick joke in the form of anonymous text messages. A rhyme, a dare, a poem - creative ways to try to push me to some breaking point.

One I didn't have.

Terminally ill kind of takes the winds out of their sails when it comes to scaring me.

Looking over my shoulder I scanned the senior hall, every face I could see without being obvious. Heritage High wasn't immune to a student body text blast yet every time my phone went off, I regretted looking.

When whispers filled the hallway, I exhaled even though it felt different this time. The whispers were normally paired with devious smiles at the Bastards but instead everyone looked worried.

They were the center of every drama and every mass text we received, yet my anonymous felt, dare I say it: *special*.

I assumed it was the upperclassman at Heritage University blessing us with the age-old tradition of "*Open Season*", but I couldn't be sure.

It was one of Heritage's oldest traditions, rumors had it was directly linked to The Brotherhood, our very own urban legend. It was their way of weeding out the losers and claiming the winners for themselves.

I'd heard about The Brotherhood my freshman year when the filter came down and I saw Heritage for what it really was: *a creepy, old town with history that ran red, run by a boy's club.*

All I wanted to do was tear down the Brotherhood before I ran out of time.

Letting the door swing shut, I carefully looked at my phone in secret while maintaining the level of not caring I had built. I hadn't wanted to look too eager, but now I couldn't stop my eyes from flying over the text.

ANONYMOUS:

> Wear all black, meet at the old barn at the edge of town, bring a flashlight and phone. No teams. No cheating. No mercy. Come and play if you dare…

I read the message over and over until the words sounded silly and misleading. *The Gathering* was no kick back and I planned on avoiding both in favor of chick flicks.

That barn was barely standing, and the threat of no mercy seemed petty compared to running around in the dark with nothing but our wits.

There was always a catch. I knew that better than anyone.

*Prognosis looks good, yet you'll still die… Every office visit with testing ended the same way… with a catch.*

Ambrose shoulder checked me, completely crashing into my concentration. The impact of his well-toned body caused me to drop my purse and everything inside it onto the glossy tile floors along with my books.

"Might want to pay attention, Clover." The way he said my name made me feel unlucky in a way the looming threat of death never could.

"Fuck you, McCall. Your ego might want to leave room for the rest of us." I snapped back before squatting down next to the mess and pushing my things back into my bag. As I reached for my phone, Ambrose pressed his boot firmly on it, forcing me to look up at him.

"Exactly how I prefer you: on your knees looking up at me with your perpetually pathetic looking eyes. Don't bother showing up tonight, I heard The Brotherhood doesn't accept *dead girls*."

Everything about him made me seethe with a white-hot rage that pulsed through my veins and circulated my whole body within seconds. Ambrose had no idea how right he was.

*No one knew.*

No, Ambrose referred to me as dead because I was nothing more than a dead girl walking, always on the other end of his torture.

Even after I started talking back, I couldn't lose the nickname.

I felt the blush spread across my tawny skin at his insult, leaving my things scattered on the floor in front of my locker, I rose to my feet. "Do they accept assholes with small dicks? Or did your daddy tell them you have a winning personality instead?"

Everyone knew his father; he had more power than he knew what to do with. Getting his son an invite to the elite secret society was the equivalent of wiping his ass with hundreds, *routine*.

A casual smile swiped across my lips like the perfect shade of lip gloss before I crossed my arms and waited for him to retreat the way I was used to now.

Before I knew it, my head was colliding with the cold metal and my eyes squinted at the sharp pain as he shoved me against my locker. Boxing me in with his arms, he got so close I swore I could feel the hate wafting off him with his expensive cologne.

He dropped his head to my ear and whispered, "I'm not playing games, Clover. If I see your face tonight, you'll fucking regret it. I'll take what I want from between those pretty thighs, and I promise you won't like it when I make *him* watch."

I swallowed hard. Ambrose promising to ruin me gave me the same butterflies he always did but I refused to react to his perfectly crafted threat.

I stood still, my head dropping to one side when I followed his eyeline directly to his brother. *Twin brother.*

Cassius McCall was the only other person forced to deal with Ambrose's punishing personality. Despite being enemy number one, I at least got a break from Ambrose when I was at home. Cassius wasn't so lucky being forced to be a part of the same fucked up family.

Judgment etched on his face in a way that got under Ambrose's skin every time I waited for Ambrose to suddenly get bored before walking away. Breaking whatever grip, he'd had on his anger. His fist slammed into the lockers behind me, the entire row vibrating under the force of his strike.

Stepping over the mess at my feet, Cassius stood at my side, the disgust almost enough to scare him off without any words. "I wouldn't want to have to tell our father about this…"

My best friend, always saving me.

That was all it took to force Ambrose to turn and walk down the hallway to his crew of fucked up pretty boys with enough arrogance to make it seem designer.

Everyone hated them.

*Lawson Ledger.*

*Magnus Gamble.*

*Gunner Baron.*

*The Boys of Heritage.*

*The Bad Royals.*

"They should have exit music, at least I could respect a theme song." I bumped my hip playfully into Cassius's, feeling the toned body he kept hidden beneath baggy shirts just to avoid the same attention his brother was subjected to.

Everyone—girls *and* guys—fawned over Ambrose and his friends.

"You didn't hear the impending doom? The breaking of teen hearts? It's screaming against my eardrums." Cassius leaned against the lockers and looked at me with emerald eyes that always made me feel at ease.

Their cruel personalities only made everyone want them more, and when they chose you... well that was a trophy no one got. It was the purest kind of initiation into their fan club.

Rumors had swirled around town that the girls they swapped around between them were branded by their mark even though no one confirmed anything. No one even knew for sure what girls made the cut.

Cassius and I had been friends since the first time his brother made me his target when I asked to sit with him at lunch. I was the new girl with no idea there was a hierarchy or his legacy status. My ignorance shot me right up to the number one spot on his hate list. Ambrose and I had been at each other's throats ever since.

Cassius was always forced to play referee, coming in and saving me at the last second.

I dropped to my knees and began picking up my things, refusing to let Ambrose ruin my day. Forcing my shoulders to relax I shoved my books in my locker after flicking the unlatched locker door open again.

"I hate him too, *Lover.*" Cassius cooed from beside me, quietly enough to feel like a secret.

Smiling sweetly at him, I let my fingers close over the fabric of his shirt and tugged him closer. Dangerously close. "I'm sure even God hates his own creation with that one."

For once, Cassius didn't laugh at my joke. He stood there tensely, his eyes drowning in mystery and his tongue swiping over his lips in this predatory way that I knew all too well.

"Lover…" The whispered name sent a tingling sensation down my spine and made me pay closer attention.

Pulling my hips toward him, our bodies collided, and I stumbled to stay upright. His hands kneaded into my hips, and the hand I had fisted into his shirt to keep my balance loosened.

He fingers toyed with my pin straight hair until it was tucked safely behind my ear. "Cassius. What are you doing? We can't—I'm not—"

All the heat between us went cold when he stood up straighter, his hands dropping from my body. "You had something in your hair. Remnants of the attack." He held up a small piece of lint between us, and I smiled softly.

I knew he was nursing a crush on me, but I didn't have the heart to tell him I only got wet for his brother.

"You're always my lucky charm." I scrunched up my nose and pouted my lips in his direction before tugging on his shirt again.

"You're the actual *Clover* here. You're the luck between us two."

I didn't feel lucky. I knew I should consider myself blessed or whatever the fuck you want to call surviving the same condition that had taken down half my family tree—at least for now…

It hadn't felt like a blessing when my mother's casket was

lowered into the ground, and everyone was able to cry on the outside the way I was weeping inside.

Hers had been a slow, painful death, and I had been forced to watch until it was over.

Now, my emotional reserve was low.

Where the capacity for tears had once been was now nothing more than a black hole. I was dried out, barren even. Whatever tears were left had turned into acid I was holding inside, poisoning the parts of me that still felt, and no amount of love or sympathy was going to cure me. So, I stopped wanting love and started wanting power instead.

Death hardens you, steals your sympathy and gives you this edge you never asked for.

I earned one scar for every year I lived without her. Each one reminded me I was alive and to keep living life with no regrets, collecting memories, and making my dead mother proud.

I was living so loudly and recklessly I hadn't even realized I'd caught the attention of Heritage's most prominent until I had gotten that text today. There had always been whispers of an elite society that ran in the shadows, behaving like royalty, but The Brotherhood was out of reach for virtually everyone. Which only made them want in even more desperately.

Cassius draped his arm over my shoulders, holding me close until we arrived at our classrooms across from each other. I was stuck with everyone we knew and hated while he got an hour break to hang out with sophomores who idealized him. I was in senior classes while he was retaking the same math class as last year because he refused to show up unless I pushed him inside the door.

Before I dipped into my class, a figure down the hall

caught my eye. It only took a moment to realize Ambrose had been watching us from afar.

Despite my best efforts, I couldn't tear my eyes away from him. His fist slamming against the lockers once more made me flinch. The sound of his anger reverberated through the now empty hallway before Ambrose turned on his heel and stalked away.

He hated that I was friends with his brother, Cassius offered a certain amount of protection no one else could. I was invincible to his brutality.

Everyone knew Cassius was in love with me and most people assumed I was his, but Ambrose didn't know I had been rejecting his brother. I kept wondering when he was going to stop calling me "*dead girl*" long enough to see that the tension between us was about to swallow us whole.

We didn't have to like each other to fuck out the hate.

Too bad he was my best friend's evil twin brother.

# Chapter 2

*Cassius*

TWO OF US were born yet only one of us mattered to our father. Ambrose decided he was going to matter to everyone else as punishment. Our father wasn't in the business of caring unless it brought him some kind of upper hand.

Unfortunately for me, I was that upper hand.

I got to be born a boy, sport the last name McCall, and be born first in the next line of heirs.

Always knowing something was off felt like the parts of my mind showboating when in reality it was my gut trying to warn me. Warn me this town was going to eat me whole, that those meds I was on kept me docile, and the constant state of fear I spotted was nothing compared to the truth.

The truth was I was being ordered to skip seeing Lover in favor of meeting the Brotherhood. Instead of convincing my best friend to take pity on me with her pussy I was the target of some power scheme.

The Brotherhood was a legend, one I always hoped existed because otherwise it was just some small town in the Carolinas not worth a damn. Now it existed and I wished it didn't.

My father broke his silence the second I turned eighteen, the moment I became eligible as their king. I only knew very little: the rules.

1. *Men only.*
2. *Women are to birth heirs and nothing more.*
3. *The breeders must die by the age of thirty at the hands of their royal.*
4. *The heirs will take their place in time of birth, down to the seconds, and the four Kings will reign supreme of the Brotherhood.*

Sounded like a bunch of bullshit, huh? I thought so too until my father told me Lover was going to be a waste of space unless I took her as a breeder.

Not a queen, not a wife, just someone to have my heir and die for it later.

It was a sure-fire way to finally make her give in to me yet when I saw her at her locker this morning all I felt was guilt. I wanted her to want me for me, not some escape ticket.

No women allowed in the Brotherhood. Every word she said I dissected, trying to figure out if she knew, if I could tell her who I was going to have to be. I was sworn to secrecy and my father made it clear broken oaths meant sacrificing my own brother.

Ambrose was arrogant, up right selfish, a total snob, and yet every night since I found out I was grateful it was me. This would have turned him into a bigger monster and the world wouldn't survive it. He lived in my unbearable shadow already, the least I could do is play the part of his unforgiving brother who made him the villain.

I was so used to playing the part he forced me too that I became blind to a lot of things. Like how he insults her, but his eyes are still undressing her. Or how he's still looking when she walks away.

My own brother was pining for my best friend, the same woman I was trying to wedge between me and my mattress. It felt like a betrayal even if it was secret.

My secrets only made us even.

All the late-night meetings about the Brotherhood left bags under my eyes and it was clear Ambrose knew nothing. All his speculation added up to the paranoia he felt as being second best in a race I wasn't trying to win.

Wanting to tell him was much different then telling him and it is becoming our next fight.

It was exhausting with someone like Ambrose who was driven by the pure need to win, demolish and destroy. He was relentless in every sense of the word.

Falling out of the doorway where I watched Clover disappear into the chem lab I stood toe-to-toe with Ambrose. "Is there a point to your outbursts or is its comic relief?" I knew my cold voice would only irritate him more.

"Wasn't it obvious? You want her and I'm going to be there to make sure you stop getting what you want." Ambrose wore that smirk perfectly, his lips just turned up enough to mean it and his eyes practically laughing.

Taking an angry step forward I crowded him, "She's not yours. She never will be."

Laughing he stood up taller, our heights matched and our features almost mirror images. "I can practically taste how greedy her pussy is for me."

Clover was supposed to be mine. I was going to be her hero, buying her power and time. The two things' people like us never got for free.

My hand found his neck without me making the command, tightening, and pushing him against the nearest wall. "Watch your fucking mouth in the presence of me. You weren't good enough for the Brotherhood and you'll never be good enough for her."

I watched his face dent and crinkle like a discarded piece of paper you ball up in your fist. All the disappointment just sitting on the surface.

"Fuck you, Cassius. You pretend to be this wounded fucking animal when you're the real monster here." He paused like the sting of his insults needed to settle in. "It doesn't matter how hard you try, no matter who you are to some fucking society, she's never going to want you. You're her best friend. I'm not going anywhere, and neither is how wet her pussy gets for me. You don't get to have everything."

My hand closed around his throat, and I felt the searing hot anger roll up my spine, joint by joining until I felt hot all over. I felt at the mercy of all the anger when I watched his gloating expression turn right into fear as my hand bared down over his throat.

It was quickly after that he started to panic, trying to loosen my grip on him and push out words I wouldn't allow. Letting my head dip into him even more I whispered, "You don't have the upper hand anymore. Everyone kneels to the Brotherhood so kneel."

Relinquishing him, his body folded forward, coughing between his legs before I pushed him over like the cheap shot it was. "*Kneel*, brother."

The anger mixed with the untapped power, and I felt invincible to my twin brother's usual torment. I finally felt in control. Just one taste of putting my bullies in line felt addictive in all the ways that I knew would be my downfall.

Pulling out my phone I snapped a quick photo of Ambrose on his hands and knees as evidence that he was obedient once, that I rise while he falls. We both knew that it was going to be the last slice of civil between us.

Swiping the screen I found the thread with my father, the sperm donor, when I typed a curt message: *I'm in but Clover is mine.*

"You think she'll like this version of you, Cas? She'll be your lucky charm while you're her bad omen?" Spitting at the floor, he stood up with a grimace that almost asked for more.

They say: *hurt people only hurt people,* but I never believed it. Not when the bullied go so silent you can't even hear their cries anymore and they don't lash out the way Ambrose did for fun.

"Then call me bad omen because she's mine and I'm king now. Your reign is over." My sharp tongue even cut the inside of my own mouth. Clover wasn't anyone's and I knew that better than anyone. She was a wild clover in a field of weeds.

The idea of her being with anyone else forced that wave of anger back up my spine and my fingers curled into a tight fist.

Ambrose stepped around me, hand patting my shoulder, "Whatever you say, brother." He was purposely mocking our relationship we didn't have, calling each other brother when it wasn't even close to what we were. "See you at the Gathering. I'm still at the table, we have the same last name, just like the same face. Remember that when she chooses me."

He didn't want her, he just wanted to make sure I didn't have her. It only made me hate him more. It only made the crown heavy I had to wear.

Another text came through from my father, lighting up the screen in my hand and drawing my eyes like a moth to a flame.

DR. MCCALL:

Yours for now. All of them die eventually.

With my face in my phone, I didn't even notice how far Ambrose had gotten, disappearing into the labyrinth we called Heritage High.

ME:

What about Ambrose?

DR. MCCALL:

He bears the same name, he still has a seat at the table, just not the crown.

ME:

I'm king now, right? I dole out punishments, right?

THERE WAS no point in trying to hide our fucked-up version of brotherly love, not even for our own father. I should have eaten him in the womb before we saw being at each other's throats after our mom died.

DR. MCCALL:

> It's inevitable, son. First you must be crowned at the ceremony. For now, you learn the rules, obligations, the commitment.

The devil you know is better than the one you don't, right? Dr. McCall, our sperm donor if I ever saw one, was a version of the devil and I didn't even realize it until I learned to play by his rules.

ME:

> How did mom really die?

I watched those three fucking dots contemplate his response for too long before they out-right disappeared altogether. The rule was that we take a woman, use them to birth an heir, and are responsible for disposing of them before they turn thirty years old. Forever cementing them as beautiful and undamaged. Before the heirs can ever truly remember them. Before we turn into little bastards with issues and trauma our doctor dad is willing to medicate until we stop caring what's wrong. Until we turned eighteen and became eligible for the Brotherhood itself.

A vicious cycle.

The devil's wet dream.

A cell with no escape.

My mom didn't die during childbirth, our father killed her because of some fucking rule that told him to. Now I wanted the truth.

# Chapter 3

*Clover*

MY FATHER WASN'T HOME when I dropped my bag at the door and kicked my shoes off. Our house was always silent and not the kind of silent that held precious memories but the kind that felt dead. My father worked overtime at the library preserving antique books and art, making us passing ships lately.

His overbearingness seemed to pull back my senior year like he knew college would drive a wedge between us. I still get multiple text messages a day reminding me how fragile I am, to take my meds, and how precious every moment is because I don't have as many as everyone else.

Before Heritage High, I was locked inside, homeschooled

and protected from even scraping my knee. I was forced to watch all the kids on my street play in the street wondering if I would ever get any scars.

Once I was granted some freedom, I vowed to collect scars, yet I found myself wandering to the kitchen, grabbing some popcorn and throwing it in the microwave instead of chasing fun at the kick back for seniors on the beach. I had the chance to chase scars and the only ones I acquired were from the oven mocking me.

The comforting pops of the kernels rattled off behind me while I mindlessly scrolled on my phone when a knock at my door startled me. No one ever came to my house; they avoided it and called me contagious my whole life. Even freshman year when I thought we were all too old for that kind of thing.

My first day of Heritage High was a nightmare of jokes, people shoving themselves into walls to avoid me in the halls, and cherry topped by Ambrose McCall making a scene when I tried to sit with him. He looked lonely when I walked up with my tray, filled with nerves, thinking we were both outcasts when he was school royalty.

He was sitting alone because everyone was afraid of him, bowing to him, not good enough to sit with him.

Pulling the door open, I saw Cassius standing there, with his obnoxiously expensive Porsche sitting along the curb. Wiggling his eyebrows, he pushed past the threshold and came inside uninvited like always. "I brought drinks. Let's celebrate my freedom."

"I thought you couldn't come." I was relieved to see Cassius and it wasn't another night alone. My eyes seemed to smile in a way I was biting down to hide.

"My dad just needed me to sign some papers, take some kind of blood oath, promise to do his bidding, and be king of some ancient cult…" His voice trailed off in the kitchen as I caught up behind him, watching him pop the tops of some beers.

Cassius was always joking, rarely serious, always using dark humor to cover up the ways I knew he felt just as alone as me.

Just like the marble surface of his body under his clothes, I had seen more of him than I bargained for. I had seen all the pill bottles acting like decor around his room, all the times I had smelled alcohol on his breath at seven in the morning when he stumbled into class, or the way he reeked of pot when he'd crawl through my window at two in the morning.

He was self-medicating the pain no one could see but him and it broke my heart, so I laughed instead of asking if he was okay. He needed me to pretend with him, so I did.

"So, a normal family night dinner?" I smiled, taking the beer from his warm hand and leaning over the counter.

Rounding the island he leaned into the edge, so close to me I could taste his cologne and beer mixing. "Things are going to change after graduation. Ambrose isn't going to bother us anymore. I promise."

Cassius sounded so full of hope that I didn't know what to do with it. I had never seen him like this, willing to talk about the future. I was the one dying, and he was more unwilling to talk about life after graduation more than me.

He was going to graduate regardless of how much class he skipped, his last name ensured that. The early acceptance to Heritage University took the weight off my shoulders of life on campus without Cassius yet he never spoke of his future.

Not until tonight with a beer in his hand and stars in his blue eyes. If you looked hard enough, you could see entire constellations.

Shrugging, forcing my eyes down at my own hands, scuffing. "He's always going to make our life miserable. Don't kid yourself, it's what he's good at."

Resting his weight into his forearms, leaning forward, and almost whispering. "I can't say anything yet... Everything is going to change. I accepted — just trust me, Lover. I just need you to say yes."

"Yes, to what, Cass?"

"Me." Standing up tall he set the beer down. "Every king needs a queen."

My brows wrinkled and my eyes lost their spark when I realized he wanted the one thing I could never truly give him, not while I loved his brother. "Cass. We have rules. Our friendship means too much to me." Pushing off the island, I ambled to the kitchen and yanked the door open on my popcorn that was still hot enough to hurt.

"This can be the same thing. We can have rules. We don't need to stop being friends. It can benefit us both." I felt his body close in on me, his height towering right behind me when his hand reached for my hip. "I have information you'll want, *Lover*. Things you need to know."

Spinning around I didn't expect him to stay planted in place when my hand landed on his chest. "Don't do that. Don't guilt me into this with information. There's nothing I need to know."

"Not even who your dad really is?" His mouth was pouty, and his voice sounded full of pity.

Letting my face warp, wrinkle, wrestle with his confessions, I crossed my arms like they would save me. "I know who he really is."

"Oh really? You think you live in this big empty house on his salary? You think your mom's mausoleum was cheap?

What about Heritage High? You could have gone anywhere but he chose private school. He's lying to you. Librarians restoring old books don't make this much money."

Shoving past Cassius I stomped to the front door, opening it and standing out of the way. "You went too far. I don't know what you promised Ambrose to get him off our backs but maybe it's not worth it."

Cassius followed close behind, stopping at the open door. "No one cares about you the way I do, Lover. I would wear a crown full of thorns if it meant protecting you. Things can be different for us, people like us. Come to the gathering tonight at the old barn. I'll prove it to you."

Flashing a small smile before he slowly moved through my front door, I forced my face to not react. I simply stood there avoiding eye contact until I could slam the door behind him.

Once the door was closed, I nearly crashed to the floor, my chest thudding so hard it felt like my ribs were cracking. My head began to spin, my eyes danced behind my eye lids and the emotional rollercoaster felt like a gut punch. Pressing my shoulders into the wall behind me I sat there, counting my breaths, and recounting my last doses of meds.

Just like clockwork I could hear the alarm on my phone blaring from the kitchen alerting me it was time for another dose. Exhaling, I stood up slowly, grasping onto everything around me until I felt my shaking legs stabilize.

I didn't even have to open a single drawer; my pink medicine box was sitting on the island right in eyesight the way my father always did before he left for work. Pressing my finger into the screen, I silenced the alarm when I saw a text message from my own father.

FATHER:

Don't forget your next dose.

ME:

Eighteen years, never missed a dose before.

FATHER:

I'm just trying to protect you, Clover.

ME:

Try overprotecting. I'm not going to die if I miss one dose.

FATHER:

Clover West you may be almost eighteen, but I will ground you until graduation. Dr. McCall works very hard to ensure we have the most time we can together.

I didn't respond, instead I simply stared at his words until they stung like the truth always does. My father and Dr. McCall were working overtime to save my life, but the Ambrose McCall's of the world were trying to kill whatever hope I had left. It lit a fire inside me that felt immortal.

I had forgotten all the way Cassius had upset me by suggesting we ruin our friendship and calling my own father a fraud. Instead, all I felt was anger that people like Ambrose got to live a long, healthy, life that he didn't deserve.

Swiping off my father's hard truths, I found Cassius's messages. He was always there, saving me and letting me collect scars the way no one else would.

ME:

Pick me up at midnight.

CASSIUS:

I'll be there, Lover. Always.

I was tired of being overprotected, I was tired of being weak, I was tired of letting Ambrose win. Cassius was offering me an upper hand and I shut him down because he knew some skeletons in my father's closet that I didn't know seemed stupid now.

Saying yes to Cassius meant taking down everyone who ever hurt us, regaining the power back after being labeled weak. I had no choice but to accept.

Give into him.

# Chapter 4

*Ambrose*

THE BLACK PAINT beneath my eyes made me feel as though someone else entirely was staring back at me from the passenger side mirror.

The perfect villain.

The same sad, twisted, angelic features I shared with my brother reflecting at myself which only made me hate him more. We were identical, yet Clover West wasn't happy with my twin's attention instead of mine and she forced me to carry that burden.

Everyone knew exactly how much my brother was in love with her and she forced me to haunt her like open season just to prove I felt nothing in return.

That greedy bitch filled her spare time with my brother and still tried her hardest to piss me off enough to chase her. I wasn't falling for it; Cassius was too fragile to survive losing her, and I wasn't about to take his place in The Brotherhood. It would be a life sentence to a group I never pledged my loyalty to the same way he did.

Cassius was older than me by three minutes, making him the next heir instead of me. I would never have to answer the call to arms our last name represented.

I sat against the cold leather that refused to warm up, shifting my line of sight off that damn side mirror. Gunner was behind the wheel, speeding down the backroads barely big enough for a single car, the cobblestone streets bullying the stability of the car.

"What crawled up your ass?" Magnus was normally the quiet threat in our group, always plotting and planning out his attacks on whatever set of panties was next. Lawson sat next to him, too smart for his own good and determined to stay the smartest guy in the room at any cost.

Dragging my eyes from the window, I shot Magnus a disgusted look over my shoulder. "Fuck The Brotherhood. I don't need it."

Magnus's closed fist struck my shoulder trying to get my attention. "What, the power? The money? The immortality? Right... no one needs that. Especially not the great *Ambrose McCall.*"

I didn't fault him for his blindness. He had lost the most of us all. Both his parents had died in a car crash on the way out of town, leaving him behind to pick up the agonizing pieces of his shattered life.

They called us every name in the book, but they should have called us motherless bastards. That's what drew us together in the first place. None of us had our mothers, except Gunner. Only his mother was under lock and key with The Brotherhood, paying off debt and Gunner was forced to watch her live through hell.

We were sons of men who didn't love anything but destruction and power.

I loved it as much as the next guy, but the kind of destruction our fathers created just created scar tissue. There were no trophies or badges of honor for what The Brotherhood did, and I was glad I wasn't in Cassius's position. I was a bomb waiting to go off, and everyone around me was tender.

"Fuck off. I don't need what I already have." I turned back around, staring back out the window until we made it to the abandoned barn on the edge of town for Open Season.

We were expected to keep up appearances, play along, and pretend we weren't legacies to The Brotherhood in order to protect their secret like all of Heritage hadn't figured it out yet.

The dirt road shook the car, my leg repeatedly bumping into the door until we came to a devastating halt. I lurched forward before catching myself with my hand on the dashboard and giving Gunner a scalding look.

Shrugging, he pulled his face into an innocent expression and tried to not laugh. It wasn't every day someone could get a cheap shot at me. Unless your name was Clover West, and I was forced to watch her flirt with my twin brother who was hopelessly into them.

No one got to see the metaphoric hits and bruises that she always left all over my fucking heart, but I couldn't break my brother just to see if Clover was worth fucking more than once. I had standards.

I climbed out of the car and stood there in my black Converse, dust already clinging to me from the disturbed dirt beneath my feet. I pulled my hoodie over my head and shoved my hands in my pockets, ignoring everyone gathering outside the barn waiting for the gunshot to go off.

Every year, a single shot was fired at midnight to signal the next round of selectees that it was time to prove their worth to The Brotherhood. And every year, I dreaded the day I would have to show up and participate.

Scanning the crowd, I saw Clover before I noticed my brother's arm draped around her shoulders like a sweater, his body pressed up against her back as he whispered in her ear.

He was forbidden from giving her any help, any hints, any truths—he knew the rules, and he was breaking them for a girl who didn't deserve it. One who wasn't going to be saved by the wrath of the bodies that were going to build his throne.

I watched them so intensely that I forgot where I was until Lawson bumped roughly into my side. "You're staring. Someone might notice you're seething when you start foaming at the mouth."

They all assumed I wanted her when I just wanted revenge. I wanted to bruise her as much as she bruised the heart inside my chest.

I rejected her, but she rejected me, too, and that wasn't something I could live with.

Cassius pressed his lips to her temple before leaving her alone in the crowd of miserable heathens looking for purpose in their lives. I watched my brother walk away, his mess of hair sitting on top of his head and his clothes hanging off him like his shoulders were merely a hanger. He walked around the barn and snuck inside while I watched him be the compliant McCall of us two. I knew Cassius would sit on the throne and inherit our father's power, and I would be forced to clean up his messes.

*His feelings.*

The same dynamic we always had.

Cassius was a mess. Emotional, off the cuff, and too nice to save his soul. Everything a cult like The Brotherhood would make sure to break first.

I followed him through the overgrown grass and silently inched into the barn. Leaning against a lone beam, I looked up at him as he donned a red robe, pulling the hood over his head. "You know you're just going to have to kill her eventually, right?"

Any woman who dared love us was committing themselves to certain death.

No woman was allowed to survive once they bore us a son to carry on the legacy. That's why we were motherless bastards growing up with men who weren't fit to raise anything but hell.

Cassius pushed his hood back down, "I'll find a way to protect her."

If we weren't twins, I wouldn't even be here. There was no preventing fate.

I couldn't contain the laughter that bubbled up my throat like vomit. He loved her enough to save her, and all of that sounded so incurable that it almost made me pity him.

I could have crushed him right there, told him how she didn't feel shit for him—at least not the way she did when I invaded her space—but I didn't. "Whatever you say, brother." Letting him live in his fantasy, I turned to rejoin the crowd I was supposed to be blending in with.

"It's *King* now."

"High off the power already, Cass?"

I left the barn without a backward glance. Staying in the shadows, I watched Clover from a distance while Cassius came into view on the second level of the barn in the cut-out where the loft was. He kept his face shrouded in darkness, commanding the crowd's attention with his scripted words. Bullshit about The Brotherhood prevailing where this town failed, the honor and privilege it was to be chosen, even though our legacies looked a lot like a curse.

None of the people here tonight were good enough to be accepted. The Brotherhood was looking for something they lost, using the people of this town to do their dirty work and weed out the pointless.

Holding the gun in the air, I watched Clover's perfect, heart-shaped mouth turn up in a grin. She wanted the one thing she would never have as long as she was a woman in Heritage... *power*.

Pulling the trigger, the shot put my eardrums in a choke-hold and not letting go until the ringing subsided, but my gaze never left Clover. I watched her run to the trucks with the tail-gates down and the beds filled with clues and supplies like she had known all along what to do.

Grabbing only an envelope, she took off in the opposite direction of everyone else in the pitch black. Curiosity guiding me, I followed her, careful to step when she did so nothing underfoot snapped into the night air. She went deep into the woods, finally stopping near the river and ripping open the envelope. Its contents spilled onto the boulder in front of her, and she ran her hands over every piece of paper before pulling out her phone.

I was close enough to see text messages flooding in and lighting her screen in the dark. I didn't bother staying quiet anymore as I approached. She was enthralled in whatever clues she was unraveling. "Don't tell me you're really trying to get in some bullshit club?"

Clover ignored me, her attention never leaving her phone even when I stood right behind her. I looked over her shoulder and saw my brother's name. *Again.*

"Cheating with Cassius?"

She scoffed and tried to hide the screen from me, but the damage was done. Whatever amount of turned on my cock felt died when I saw his name again.

"It's not cheating. He only told me to head toward the water and look for something out of place. And look at that... the town reject fell right into my lap. Couldn't be more out of place, Ambrose."

She must have been pleased with her quick wit to smile so proudly. Rounding the boulder, I sat down on her clues. "The Brotherhood isn't impressed easily, Clover. It's going to take more than that pretty fucking mouth of yours."

Breaking down her walls was easy. Too easy. The slightest amount of attention, and she melted into a puddle of heat and wetness.

"Don't be jealous you'll never know from personal experience," she retorted.

I stood, closing the space between us until our chests collided with every jagged breath, we took against the cold night air.

"Keep teasing me, Clover, it only makes me want to ruin you sooner than I planned." Leaning down, I stoked the fire I knew I started within her and tucked a piece of hair behind her ear. I exhaled softly over the sensitive skin of her neck.

*Something I shouldn't know but did.*

*Something Cassius didn't know.*

*Something that was all mine.*

"Cassius would never forgive you." Her throaty voice barely contained a threat, yet it sent shame down my spine.

She was right. My brother would never forgive me for taking what he had claimed as his own. Even though Clover West was the only person who didn't pay any mind to his innocent crush.

She didn't take a single step back or try to protect her space in any way. She stood there unmoving; our bodies pressed against each other. Forcing a laugh, I made sure she felt small before I continued, "I'm not afraid of Cassius."

"He's going to have more power than you do. *Spoiler alert:* you peak in high school." Her curt voice sliced through my exterior.

Our faces were so close I could see the pulse in her delicate veins in her neck. Inching closer I locked eyes with her, our mouths nearly brushing in a way that woke up my cock again. "I promise you; I'll break his heart before you do. That's better than power. I'm gonna destroy him and force you to watch him come undone. Not even your tight little pussy is going to save him then."

I paused to let my words sink in, then pivoted into the night, mourning what could have been if Cassius wasn't wedged between us, forcing me to take into account how truly fragile he was.

A boy pretending to be a man wearing a crown. We both knew he was going to fail at that too. It was only a matter of time before my father saw who the real heir was.

Even if it was the last thing I wanted.

I didn't want the fucking crown; I didn't want the headache, but I wanted her, and I couldn't have a damn inch. Making sure he couldn't either was the only objective here.

# Chapter 5

Clover

AMBROSE THOUGHT he was so cunning with his smile that could kill and the way his voice got low like he was hypnotizing you. He had me wrapped around his finger until his brother offered me power, privilege, and a life that I could abuse until I eventually died.

All the possibilities.

All the scars.

All the ways I could claim I lived.

He tormented everyone around him mercilessly and now it was his turn to suffer. Cassius and I didn't see eye-to-eye on letting our friendship be anything more than friendship, but we agreed on this. Making sure they knew exactly how it felt to live in their shadows.

Him and his royal court backing every threat he ever doled out.

Cassius kept a tight lid on how things were going to change for us. Only telling me that I would become invincible the second I said yes that I would be his queen. None of it made sense, hell, nothing made sense anymore but once you see something shiny everything else becomes background.

I didn't care how it was going to work - I just wanted my prize.

I wanted to wear a crown. I wanted real scars. I wanted revenge.

Karma is a bitch but so was I.

# Chapter 6

*Cassius*

NO ONE COULD KNOW that Clover knew as much as she did. She barely scraped the surface of the Brotherhood, and it was already too much.

Not even the women carrying our heirs could know the details in demonic. They had to have blind trust and that's what made them targets in the end.

Good enough to bear an heir but not an ounce more.

She had to pretend to care at the Gathering. She had to pretend she had a chance of getting into the men's club. She had to trigger Ambrose into starting a war. Breaking him was only worth it if he fought back, there's no point in putting down a dying dog.

I waited behind the bar, standing in the pitch black and pinching a blunt between my fingers. Sucking in the high I felt my chest tighten as I held my breath, grasping the way the edge was being shaved off.

"Lover? Is that you?"

I couldn't make out any silhouettes in the dark even with my eyes focused down into slants.

"Try again. Haven't you gotten beat up enough, Cass? When are you going to learn it doesn't matter what you do... you're damaged. You're never going to be us." Magnus, the football star riding his scholarship all the way to the pros, stepped close enough for me to make out features.

"You have to *bow*. I'm about to be your *king*." I snorted back, exhaling around my words. I wasn't afraid of Ambrose's friends doing his dirty work.

Athlete sounded like an insult to the amount of muscle Magnus spotted. He was solid stone and if I cared about that kind of thing, I could imagine I would have cowarded. "I don't bow to anyone, *bitch*. Let's try to learn our lesson one last time."

My body flew back so casually, hitting the barn, that it felt natural. It wasn't until his punishment came barreling down in fists that felt soul crushing.

The blunt fell from my fingers and the pain stomped out any kind of high I was riding. He was on repeat: kick, punch, kick, punch until I curled up against the barn wall and clamping my eyes closed.

Things were supposed to be different. Being king, saying yes to every bad thing they were going to ask me to do felt worth it but now it all became clear that nothing was going to change.

We were playing games out of our league, pretending to be

royally untouchable when we were totally fucked. People like Ambrose are born to rule, not me.

I don't know when Magnus gave up, the throbbing echoed all over my body long after he was gone. Laying there I tasted the metallic blood inside my mouth, and it took every ounce of effort to collect it, spitting it out on the overgrown grass surrounding the broken-down barn.

Lighter footsteps seemed to grow closer when I dragged myself backwards, clawing at everything to disappear into the night. Finally hidden behind the door I held my breath until I heard Clover's voice cascade through the air. "Cassius? Are you here?"

We were supposed to meet here but I wasn't supposed to be battered the way I was. I didn't want to give her a reason to say no. To run into his arms instead.

Pulling out my phone between my legs I leaned against the wall and texted her a message to meet at my house in two hours instead. Enough time to look like my normally damaged self instead of the trash I felt like.

THE HOT SHOWER only did so much to the already forming bruises when I wrapped the towel low on my waist. Standing in the mirror all I saw staring back was distortion, pieces of me that didn't line up, just like all those pieces my father was hell-bent on fixing.

Swiping my palm through the fogged-up mirror, I saw the red marks and light purple bruises come into focus around my ribs. By the time my eyes scanned up to my face I could see the bruise over my cheekbone only exaggerating the sharpness.

Carefully, I touched my face, smoothing over the mark like it would somehow force it into hiding before Clover got here.

My tongue rolled over my bottom lip catching a new wound when I felt the sting jolt through me. Bracing my hands on the counter I sighed out loud in disappointment.

I should have been untouchable now, yet Magnus had touched every vulnerable spot I had and left a mark to prove it. Thankfully our father worked late and had the Brotherhood to keep him preoccupied. Enough to not see how he picked the wrong son.

Nothing was going to change. Losers would stay losers.

Opening the bathroom door hanging off my room, I felt the cold air prick my skin when I jumped back against the molding. I didn't expect to see Clover sitting on my bed reading the journal next to the bed, so entrenched she didn't even look up.

"That's private you know." I forced myself to forget the pain of walking when I sat down next to her.

Without looking up she responded, a tear falling to the page and bleeding. "It's beautiful."

My little black book was filled with poems and drawings instead of girl's numbers. I had no check marks on my bed posts, all I had was the girl sitting in my bed reading poems about herself.

Taking the book away from her I forced her to look at me. Gasping at my bruised covered body she clamped her hands over her mouth. "Cassius."

My jaw ticked with tension. "Magnus didn't like our little stunt. Fucking bastards."

Scooting closer to me, she sat at my side with her legs folded up like a pretzel, reaching out to touch me. Flinching against the one person I pinned for she whispered. "It's just me…"

"It's never just that simple, Lover. It's always been you. Even when it's not me."

Her eyes were floodgates threatening to fall when our eyes met, and her hand paused in the air between us. "I want it to be you. I'm saying yes. I want this."

Pushing her hand down to her legs I rejected every part of her finally giving in to me. "Don't. It's not nice to kick a dog when he's down."

Getting up I tossed the small leather notebook on my night-stand before I stood there unsure where to go from here. Everything fell apart before it even got to begin.

Clover dropped her legs down, dangling off my bed that sat high off the floor before pinching the zipper on her hoodie. Dragging the zipper down, giving me a glimpse of her tawny skin and the charm hanging from the center of her bra.

So that's what was under that hoodie. Just a pink bra meant to torment me.

"I said *yes*, Cassius." Slipping off the bed she stood between me and the bed, shrugging off the hoodie until it fell to the floor. Her hand reached for my towel still clinging to my hips. "Tonight, doesn't have to be a failure…"

Her soft hands undid my towel, letting it drop and not deviating her eyes off mine. Her green eyes glowed in the dim lighting of my messy room. It was a collision course of debris, the old me who seemed happier and freer, and this new version who showed up after puberty.

It only made the critical voices living in my head worse. I was punishing myself for not being that person anymore by looking at all the things I used to love.

*Love.*

That word, that feeling, was something I only reversed for Clover because she couldn't hurt me. Not when she didn't let me ruin the friendship. Not like this, right now.

Her fingers danced down my chest and the tension were almost too much to take. "What if this ruins us?" Taking a step closer I forced her to touch me more in a desperate kind of way.

"I can't think of a better way to ruin our friendship than letting you take my virginity..." Her emerald eyes nearly spoke directly to my hard cock.

Dropping my head down enough to reach her lips we collided. A rush skated down my spine when my hands instinctively curled around her hips, pulling her closer to me.

Her body was on fire, hot to the touch when I fought with the claps of her bra and ripping off the material quick enough to close my mouth over hers again. My tongue licked her lips, prying them open before searching the inside of her mouth.

A small moan erupted from her mouth, humming right into mine. Yanking at her hips, pulling her closer before my hand disappeared between us. Cupping her pussy through her jeans I made her purr again by digging my thumb against the seam.

"I don't know what you like," her breathy voice pushed through our kissing.

Keeping our mouths wrestling I took her hands in mine, dragging it down my chest until she was dangerously close to my cock.

"What I like?" I took a hard swallow, not even sure myself. I hadn't toyed with the idea of anything else but her and my hand. Now that isn't a firm grip, I know all too well all I could come up with was: "You."

Her hands weren't nervous like mine and her mouth was hungry for more when her lips nipped at mine. Taking my hands in hers and placing them over her bare tits. "I'm not gonna break, Cassius. You can fuck me the way you always wanted to."

The naughty words rolled off her tongue while my fingers pinched her nipples until they were hard enough to bite. Pushing her back onto the bed I took her nipple hostage, letting my tongue assault her and my teeth pretend to hurt her. Because I wasn't any different than anyone else, we break the things we love the most. To be the destroyer? So, no one else can, have it? Because we can? All my pulsating cock wanted was to make her cry.

I wanted to be the reason Clover West cared. I wanted to finally get behind those walls and if the door was between her legs, then I was going to be the key.

Her moans were raspy echoes when I trailed playful bites down her ribs, unbuttoning her jeans, and ripping them down her legs. Her panties were so thin the material was soaked through, and it only made my cock jump.

"You're already wet for me?" It was a rhetorical question, but I still wanted to hear her say it, that I was the reason. "Say it, Lover. Tell me I'm why you're so fucking wet."

Clover arched her back letting her head fall to the side and her tongue darted out, licking her lips. "You're why..." her words disappeared to pleads for more.

I could feel those walls still erected and between us, just like I was.

My fingers slipped under the elastic band of her underwear pulling them down her legs until I could ball them up. Tucking them between my mattress and box spring for safe keeping.

Lazily I stroked myself, not that I needed help, I was rock hard and pulsing so much it felt like the worst cock tease. All of me needed to be inside all of her.

Climbing the bed, she pushed herself further up the bed until she found the stack of pillows that hadn't been washed in months. I banished the maids from entering my room and policing whatever illicit behavior I felt like that day.

Our thighs touched and my mouth went dry instantly. Clover's legs were crossed at the ankles like I hadn't memorized the exact shade of pink her pussy was and exactly how glossy she was.

"Do you have a condom?" Her voice whispered into the crook of my neck.

Reaching over to the small lamp, I reached in the drawer and fished one out, the only one. Ambrose threw it at me during one of his infamous parties telling me to fuck it instead of ever thinking it would be Clover. His insult turned ironic now that she was mine.

Turning off the light I watched the room turn into shadows when I sat back on my heels, wrestling with the material and groaning at my own touch. "Fuck," sang from my mouth. Sitting up Clover started kissing my neck, my jaw, my throat until that pit in my stomach threatened to go up in flames. "Lover... baby girl... I can't focus on putting this shit on while you're doing... that."

Straddling my lap, her arms wrapped around my neck, her mouth marking every inch of my skin still. "I trust you, *Ambrose*."

The paranoia I always felt spiked. My face was dipped in ecstasy only to be ironed out. I must have misheard her. "*Ambrose?*"

Straddling my lap, her hips swayed, and her labored breathing begged to be abused by my thickness. "What are you talking about? It's me, I want you."

The sincerity in her voice forced me to let it go when I brushed my tip against her clit, stretching her pussy enough to fit. Her body went rigid on top of me, halting all movements. "It's so big…" her voice rattled uncontrollable as she inched down on me.

Ignoring any mistake, she may have just made I felt the anger boil up inside me. That pit of my stomach was suddenly hot for other reasons.

Slamming her hips down I punished her with every thick inch burning her pussy, bending her will and forcing her to stretch for me. My fingers laced through her hair, grasping onto the roots and forcing her head back. "Nothing's been inside this tight pussy? Not even a toy?"

Gasping, her mouth opens carelessly, she shook on top of me. "No… no… just my fingers." She could barely put the words together, almost speechless.

"Good girl. Now ride me." The anger of the truth mixed with the regret of turning our first time into punishment kept me distracted.

I always knew. Clover West was infatuated with my brother, yet nothing ever came of it because he was more closed off then she was. Instead, I played along, being her best friend, waiting for her to see I wouldn't hurt her the way he would.

None of that mattered, when it came down to it, she still moaned his name.

She was his, no matter what I did, and it made me hate her for not seeing me. Not even with every fucking inch of me making her wetter.

Digging my hands into her ass I grunted, letting my teeth grind, and my jaw got knotted up. Her eyes clamped shut and the rage inside of me ripped through my composed surface.

She was picturing him. Maybe not picturing since we were mirror images, but she was pretending I was him.

She was fucking my brother, not me.

The awkward, nervous entertainment I once embodied as she yanked my towel down was nothing but pure, untapped, madness. My hands weren't soft anymore, my mouth kissed her like it needed to hurt, and I wouldn't let her hips ride up on me enough to feel any relief.

If she wanted to pretend, I was Ambrose I was going to force her into coming the same way he would.

Clover West lost the privilege of me. She'd lose my protection too, but we made a deal. Clover West was mine. She wanted mean, and now she was going to get it.

# Chapter 7

*Clover*

THE COME DOWN of what Cassius and I did crawl all over my body for weeks. I couldn't seem to forgive myself for the mistake I made.

I slept with my best friend and none of it ignited some kind of love story. It was just sex; it was just a mistake that felt right in the moment.

Single handedly ruining our friendship I avoided my best friend like he suddenly came down with the plague. I was looking around corners, skipping the classes I didn't need to go to, and praying for time to speed up to graduation so I wouldn't have to face him.

Cassius McCall took my virginity, and I wished it was his brother.

Everyone saw Cassius unravel after that night, after the gathering and Magnus beating him to a pulp. He stopped hiding all his bad habits, going around telling people he was royalty now, and showing up drunk to school.

Driving his car nearly into the chem lab really tipped off everyone that Cassius had really gone over the edge. The worst part is that it was all my fault.

I watched him kill himself right in front of me and yet I was still hiding in the shadows, ashamed of what we did. I had said yes to power, to his plan, to whatever it took, and I was taking back every word. I was just hoping our friendship survived it.

Cassius wasn't at school when I scanned the hallways and parking lot for his vintage Porsche. Inhaling a big gulp of air, I felt my shoulders relax some when my mind refocused.

Magnus Gamble beat up my best friend all because we craved their status. They were scared and lashing out before all their power evaporated. Before we took it all away.

It may have been a mistake to let Cassius slip between my legs so easily, but I knew exactly how to fix it - making sure Magnus paid for what he did. I was going to protect Cassius for once.

Holding my head higher I stopped looking around the next corner for Cassius. I had a plan, I had a purpose, and whatever happened I could plead that our friendship never stopped mattering.

Opening my locker, I ran through all the ways I could hurt the people who claimed to be invincible. The stampede of hurried footsteps only got louder when some nameless outcast threw a stack of papers in the air before running from getting caught. The paper sliced across my bare leg before landing before my feet. Carefully bending down in my leather skirt, I plucked the page up from the ground before reading all the ways it broke the rules.

In bold letters far too big for the page it was an open invitation to the royal's graduation party. Wasn't it generous of them to invite everyone who doesn't measure up?

Rolling my eyes, an idea nearly knocked me over and showed up in a grimace. That was exactly how I was going to get them back. Everyone would be fawning over them, begging for their attention and I was going to steal it.

I wanted to text Cassius, I wanted to drive to his house and watch him come alive at the thought of our plan working yet I let my hand drop to my side with my palm hugging my phone.

Closing my fist around the cold screen I was determined to win him over, erasing that night from our memories. Letting my locker close behind me I pivoted on the ball of my feet to only be met with Ambrose standing there sullen.

"Just the person I'm looking for. My homewrecker." He stepped forward demolishing all boundaries. "What kind of game are you playing? Breaking him before I could... I'm impressed by your stupidity. That's not how I wanted to break him."

Scuffing at his poor attempt at intimidation I steeled my spine and crossed my arms. "Do you always have Magnus do you dirty work? Now... be honest, does he suck your dick too or was that the prize for doing what you couldn't?"

You could visibly see the way Ambrose's jaw grinded, the way his eyes filled with anger enough to cloud how crystal blue they were, and his hands begged to squeeze the life out of me so much his knuckles turned a shade of ironic.

Towering over me he stepped into me enough that I backed

right up into my locker, rattling the metal against the excitement. I should have been afraid; I should have panicked the way I always did but Cassius wasn't here to save me.

I had to save myself and that meant realizing I didn't have time to be scared. I had a friendship to save and illness to beat.

Cassius dangled power in front of me and it felt better than love.

"Real fucking cute." His tongue assaulted his bottom lip the way I wanted him to assault the thin cotton of my panties. "You'll never be anything but his slave. In fact, you'll be the one sucking his dick as a prize. The Brotherhood comes first, no matter how good you think that tight pussy is. You like the taste of power? Get on your knees and swallow some real power down. Cassius is a broken king, I'm a fucking God."

His hand on my shoulder pinched my skin until I toppled over to one side. My eyes pricked at the thought of failing to stand up to him.

"Is God supposed to taste stale?" Moving my mouth around the invisible bad aftertaste I continued, "Or is that a personal choice?"

The hand that was on my shoulder moved quickly to my throat and that panic I swallowed was working its way back up my throat. "You'll regret that when you realize after I break that crown."

I believed every word. I knew he was going to break his brother, but I had no idea where their hate started.

"Why do you hate him so much? Why can't you just leave us alone."

I don't know what made me look around Ambrose when I noticed the entire senior hallway was frozen in place. Every set of eyes fixed on us and my whole body went up in flames.

I felt burned at the stake even more when Ambrose

abruptly stepped back and gave everyone a clearer view of me. It was almost like he had done nothing wrong when everyone's eyes stuck to me, and his smirk confirmed everything everyone already thought *freak*.

Outcast, freak, loser - so many ways to say the same shit. Whatever Ambrose and his friends declared. Could be worse I guess... Billie Tetro was declared a slut after some party I wasn't invited to, Cassius was declared mental, and the rest of the student body wore name tags they created.

No one questioned it, we all just waited for someone else to be their next target. Unfortunately, for me it was my turn.

Magnus stood off the row of lockers across from us, slow clapping, grinning from ear to ear. "Tell your boyfriend they have meds for that. For the damage I did, not the bruised ego."

I hated Magnus. I hated him more for what he did and whatever came after hate? That was surging through my veins like laced drugs. The happiness sitting on his lips as he clapped for taking one of us down.

Starting a rumor wasn't enough. Embarrassing them wasn't enough. I wanted to ruin their lives and that's exactly what I was going to do. With or without Cassius.

I TOOK one last look reflecting back at me in the window of my car, swiveling my hips to make sure everything was hugging the right curves. I wanted to feel lethal; not terminal.

My phone blared through any confidence I was feeling when it shouted at me to take my medication before a slew of symptoms shot through me like a bad nightmare. The last time

I forgot, I had a seizure in the middle of the hockey field and Ambrose took every opportunity to point out the flaw in design.

Letting it slip my mind entirely I fished out the small, round, pills from my mini purse. Popping open the pill case and dry swallowing my medicine that wasn't curing anything at all.

I wanted so badly to throw them out and just let myself die but all of that faded quickly when I found a purpose in avenging my best friend. Now I wanted to outlive them all.

Sitting into that feeling I stood up straighter, letting my heels put me on the pedestal. I felt brand new, the anger filling all the voids and cracks. Strutting up his driveway I pushed the sunglasses on my face before I made it to the door.

Stopping at the threshold I waited for the hooligans smoking outside to pull the door open in a silent demand. Ambrose was waging a war and I had to soldier up to win.

My sunglasses sat just low enough for my eyes to scan the room without the tint when I shrugged off my sweater, exposing the sheer shirt that was barely long enough to be considered a dress. I could feel the eyes on me, only this time it was for a whole other reason than earlier in the hallways.

I stood in the entryway, letting people look, letting the attention force my nipples to pinch up under the black shirt free of any material underneath.

Pivoting, I made my way to the kitchen where the music seemed to drown out in comparison. The kitchen was dark, the bottles of hard liquor all half drank and familiar.

Cassius wasn't a stranger to drinking himself to sleep and I wasn't a stranger to taking care of him when he crossed that thin line.

Leaning against the counter I crossed my ankles and

scanned the room for the bad royals, the bastards, when I spotted Magnus tilting a pink cup upside down.

I took out my phone, pretending to text when I knew I had no one to text but the one person mad at me. Holding the screen close enough I prayed he texted me anyways.

Smiling to myself I thought out a whole conversation: *this party blows, come to the pool house, come to my room, save me from the horror* but nothing comes through.

Their house was huge, the kind of huge that made you feel part of the decor, blending right into the luxury instead of owning it. It was a lot different than crawling through Cassius's window.

My eyes darted around without my head moving, examining the cold environment that produced two very different people when Magnus flocked to my flame exactly how I wanted. Letting my head drop to the side, away from him like a cold shoulder I waited for him to speak.

I watched him set his lip free from under his bite out of the corner of my eye. "Are you new in town?"

Magnus Gamble, the single hand defense against getting scored on (on and off the field), didn't recognize me. Not hard to do when you pretend to be a ghost your entire life just to make grieving me easier. Only now there was no one to grieve. Only Cassius and even that was on shaky ground.

Shaking my head up and down I decided to not speak unless I had to. I was going to ride his ignorance all the way home.

"Let's get out of here," he purred. Taking a big step into me, his big hands hugging my hip, and his cologne was wafting me in the face.

I let him take my hand, leading me away from everyone, away from the safety in numbers if he recognized me after all.

Shouting to myself I let the mask slip right back into place, I had to commit, I had to pretend I wasn't a living dead girl the way Ambrose teased.

Playing pretend was easy. I did it my whole life. Every time I watched the neighborhood kids play outside, I would sit at the window pretending I had better things to do, declining their offer, and making up stories as I watched them in jealousy. Pretending to not be sick, pretending I was going to live past thirty and break my family's curse.

I had a lot of practice.

Magnus was just another way I would pretend.

# Chapter 8

## Clover

EVERY STRAY BRANCH snapped under my heels, and I could feel debris scratching at my skin while Magnus dragged me behind him through the woods.

From this angle, Magnus looked like a monster who lived in the woods, a stalking shadow that didn't have to haunt you. You were destined to be his prey.

With a gentle yank I collided into him, feeling his hands guide my back into a thick trunk of a tree. I could feel the roughness of the bark clearly contrasting with Magnus's entire personality. It only made what I was about to do even worse.

His mouth took mine hostage, his tongue licking the seam of my lips before forcing his way inside my mouth. A few seconds of sloppy kissing before he pulled just enough away to speak, "Just tell me to stop…" Trailing off I felt the sting of guilt prick down my spine.

Magnus was the kind of guy who asked for consent, and I was biting my lip at how sexy it felt to have someone ask.

I had just lost my virginity in the world's most awkward way, clamping my eyes down the whole time and pretending it wasn't a mistake enough to not hurt my best friend. Joke's on me - I hurt him regardless.

I had no choice but to avoid him until the glaring truth of seeing each other naked didn't make me blush in embarrassment.

Nodding my head up and down I committed to not speaking, not letting him recognize me. Feeling for his hands I smoothed them up my body until stopping at my neck. With a hard swallow I squeezed his callous skin until my mouth fell open in a clear approval.

"You're one of those freaky girls?" He smirked, tightening his grip. "Good, I'm one of those guys too."

Finally, I had done enough to force Magnus to show his true colors, exactly why everyone called them bad royals.

I felt the tightening around my throat forcing me to take shallow breaths and my chest to pound in response as his mouth kissed my face. My eyes threatened to close when his sneaker kicked at the inside of my foot, separating my legs.

The adrenaline came out as a breathy moan. I wanted more of his abuse, I wanted to know exactly how far he would go.

I had surprised myself; I didn't want to be treated like a delicate flower like Cassius did. I wanted the scars of living before I died.

My ability to breathe turned only into pants as my panties soaked through. The moisture coated my inner thighs and I felt bad in a way that felt better than the power Cassius promised. "Harder," I demanded.

Magnus stilled, his eyes catching mine and assessing the damage before his grip around my neck choked any last sense he had to stop. "You wanna be my good little bitch? Turn around."

Comfortable enough to make demands he let my neck go free and the chill of the night air kissed the heat I was still wearing. Twisting around I nearly tripped over my own feet breaking my landing before my face did it for me. Standing against the tree, heaving to get fresh air to fill my lungs as he kicked my legs apart again.

"Stick your ass out."

Without any warning, but the material of his jeans wrestling against his skin, I let the excitement stir between my legs. Suddenly the smooth sound of his belt sprinting through his belt loops rang in my ears and I knew exactly what was coming next...

The genuine leather of his belt crushed against my unblemished thighs right below my ass and I winced at the pain with a smile tugging at my lips.

I didn't want to be caressed, I wanted to be fucked the way Cassius was afraid to.

Eating up the burn I stuck my ass out more when his crotch pushed up against my ass and I could feel the outline of his hard dick in his jeans. Letting my hips roll the friction against my fresh wound made me bite down on my moans.

"Just like that. Tell me how badly you wanna be fucked like a slut in the woods. I wanna hear you scream so loudly they all hear you." Flicking the edge of my shirt up his hands forced my hips still.

I wanted to speak but I couldn't unless I wanted to blow

my cover. We were already dangerously close to the threshold of the manicured lawn, just beside the pool house, close enough to get caught.

That wasn't an option. I needed him to think this was our little secret.

Choking, I snapped up right, my fingertips dancing along my neck when I felt his belt loop around my neck. Pulling back on the leather his mouth caught my ear again. "I can't hear you."

All the tension, excitement, all the arousal dripping down my legs felt like panic. True panic.

I hadn't planned to be trapped.

My spine curved against the taunt belt he was tugging on when my purposely dropped phone rang out with the alarm I set. Illuminating in the dark he seemed to lose focus when his hand dropped, and I gasped for air.

Pressing my cheek against the cold tree I let my chest expand and deflate all too quickly. My fingertips feeling up my own neck to wear the belt had choked every good sense out of me.

"I should go…" I whispered as I gathered the strength to walk away, not even mentioning dropping my phone.

Carefully, I undid the belt that had nearly threatened to tear a new whole through the leather just to permanently fit around my neck. I felt owned by him, and the sleek kind of torture still pumped through my body as a reminder before I dropped the belt on the ground.

My legs were shaking, and I could still feel the belt around my neck like it was still there. With every step I put between us I could feel his anger. "Hey bitch! What am I supposed to do now?"

"Figure it out," I shouted as I kept walking.

Plucking up my discarded phone I held it in my hand and smiled.

Making him mad was just a perk when I tipped toed through the abandoned woods, stepping on the manicured lawn. Slipping off my heels I headed the opposite direction of the party. Sneaking into the pool house I dropped myself down on the couch in the dark.

I couldn't shake Magnus. I couldn't shake his touch, the way his hot breath made me feel on fire, the way his rough hands felt against my smooth skin.

Clamping my eyes down for just a second I let myself enjoy it, enjoy the enemy. Biting my lip, I rubbed my legs together enough to scratch the itch of his memory. Cutting myself off I swiped the lock screen away and brought up the keypad to make a call.

Heritage Crisis Hotline.

It was enough to get him in trouble, enough to have them call the cops instead of me. It was the perfect next move in ruining his life. All those scholarships were about to be rescinded, his football career put on hold for assault, and all the ways he called himself a freak weren't going to seem so kinky when every girl in Heritage gave him the cold shoulder.

I was going to make Magnus a cancer everyone cut out to save their own asses.

A soft voice on the other end answered, "Crisis line, this is Lark."

I expected something else entirely when I held my breath so vigorously that my eyes watered on command. "I need to - I need to talk to someone. Can you hear me? I'm at Ambrose McCall's party... I think I was just assaulted..."

I sat there, my back against the couch that was slippery and meant to wick away moisture. I waited for her to respond when her obvious shock rendered her silent.

"Can we start with your name? Why do you think you were assaulted?"

The floodgates of tears streamed down my face as I responded with exaggerated pauses and hitches in my voice. "He had his belt around my neck... I couldn't say no. I couldn't move; he was too strong."

"Do you know who did this to you? I'm going to call the police on the other line. Stay with me."

"Magnus Gamble. I'm positive."

The other line was audible when I heard the unmistakable voice announce that she had called Heritage's finest. More like worthless. They were funded by the Brotherhood everyone whispered about and that meant anyone not worthy wasn't taken seriously.

I was going to make it impossible for them to cover up anything anymore.

Hanging up the phone abruptly I held it in my hands and let myself be pleased with myself when the door opened, and I froze. I expected to see Magnus ready to strangle me into coming when I sunk down into the couch trying to blend into the darkness.

Almost holding my breath, I watched the figure move so gracefully he must have known the layout of the pool house. He pulled off his shirt, his broad shoulders and toned body reflecting the tinkle lights hanging on the outside before grabbing a towel and throwing it over his shoulder.

Licking my lips, I couldn't take my eyes off him. In one seamless motion I watched Ambrose take down his pants before kicking them aside.

Ambrose McCall, my enemy, my rival, was standing stark

naked in front of me after I had ruined his best friend's life in the name of his brother. It was complicated but it didn't make it any less alluring.

The hard swallow against my dry throat almost hurt when he looked over his shoulder. "You're trespassing. It's the only rule of my parties: no pool house."

Sitting up in the dark I pressed my elbows into the tops of my thighs. "Aren't rules supposed to be broken?"

"Not mine, *dead girl*." He refuted.

"Cute, you recognize my voice even in the dark."

Turning around he left the towel hanging over his shoulder. Not one ounce of shame, he was proud of everything his body was and I could see why without the extra saliva pooling in my mouth. "Don't you know? Cassius doesn't come to these. Or are you finally upgrading?"

"Upgrading to what? Your loser friends who think they run things?"

Stepping closer, around the furniture and dropping down in the chair across from me he let his legs fall open. I had an up close and personal view of every endowment, and I couldn't help but compare.

Cassius was beautiful but Ambrose was something else entirely. Every part of him was made of pedigree, persistence and privilege.

No one in their right mind was going to sit down naked and carry on a conversation yet Ambrose took that challenge. "Eyes up here, sweetheart."

Rolling my eyes, I looked away while he adjusted the towel to land over his crotch. Continuing he smirked between words, "We do run shit. You hate me and you still can't keep your eyes off me. That's what I call power, *dead girl*."

"Or pity. Whatever you prefer," I quipped.

He leaned forward and even with the space between us I still sat back trying to maintain the space between us. "Open those legs. Let's see how much pity is making that pussy wet."

My face went up in a dishonorable scarlet at his asking to see my wet panties as proof I was worshiping the power, he had over me.

"That's power, Clover. Not whatever bullshit Cassius is selling you."

Ruining Magnus was underway, Gunner and Lawson next on mg hit list but Ambrose was the kind of royalty that wasn't ruined by a scandal. He had power, whether I wanted to admit it or not.

Ambrose McCall was always going to have the power. Until I took some back.

Pushing my knees apart I sat back until my shirt crept up my legs and he had the perfect view of my panties. "He's convinced you'll leave us alone. That some crown is going to finally put you in your place. He's not going to let you push him around forever. High school is practically over then what? Become a college bully?"

I watched his eyes squint down into an emotion I never saw on his face before. *Vulnerability.*

"How do you think I got like this, Clover? Someone had to be strong. Someone had to be fucking sane. Someone had to be all the shit he refused. And guess what? They still picked him. That fucking crown he thinks will change things. It will change everything. It's not gonna save any of us, it's damnation. Dead girls don't care about dying. Cassius won't survive it." His confession might have been the most words he ever spoke to me that weren't laced with insult after insult.

"You're blaming Cassius for you being an asshole?"

Falling next to me he pushed my leg into my other leg

66

lazily, "Wishing you were never born breeds a perfect asshole. Not a twin brother mad at you for being the better version."

"Wow," I exhaled in disbelief. "Is anything you say genuine? Do you have feelings? Cassius hasn't been to school in a week, and you don't even blink an eye."

His head dropped to the left; eyes boring into me. "Whose fault is that really? You not loving him or mine?"

Shame wrapped around every limb and suddenly I felt weak instead of strong. "Who says I don't love him?"

Ambrose pushed his face towards mine, closing in on me and only stopping when his mouth was dangerously close. "Your pussy, the way you looked at me, the way you know every difference between us, exactly how badly you want me to kiss you right now."

"I'm protecting him from everything that will hurt. Including you. Someone must be the asshole, Clover, so I'll be the villain. He can't take the crown and he's not going to listen to anyone but you."

Squirming in place I licked my lips. "How do I know that's not some trick?"

Scuffing, his head shook in disbelief. "I don't want the crown. I don't need the brotherhood. I have everything I could ever want."

I wanted him to need me.

I wanted him to say something real, not riddled with innuendos and veiled threats.

"I'm glad you have everything you need."

Leaning further into me his lips nearly caressed mine. I thought I hallucinated it until I started to speak, my mouth open while my brows wrinkled trying to produce words.

"Shut the fuck up, Clover. You're going to save my brother, wanting you isn't an option." Our mouths crashed together like feral animals and mouse hands reached out to grab any part of each other that we could. Nothing was enough when our tongues finally fucked the way I wanted him to fuck me.

None of this was a good idea.

None of this made any sense. We were enemies, now rivals, making out in his pool house in the dark.

I was supposed to be avenging Cassius by destroying his brother and friends for making his life hell. I wasn't avenging anything, and I was losing the war for my panties tonight.

The shame never came when Ambrose pushed me back against the couch and climbed on top of me. My lips felt sore from all the kissing, yet I didn't want it to stop.

Ambrose might be a *friend* now but tomorrow he was going to be my rival. This changed nothing, not when I had a plan to destroy him.

# Chapter 9

*Cassius*

LOCATION SERVICES SHOWED Clover at my house. Following the blue dot on the map of my own property I ended up at the pool house, a safe distance away from the party, sitting beyond the pool.

It was almost quiet when I walked up to the glass doors, a sheet of thick darkness inside. Pressing my face to the glass I cupped my hands around my eyes when I saw my brother mauling my best friend.

Clover wasn't exactly fighting him off from under his mouth. His hands were gripping her breasts through her shirt and whatever awkwardness we shared seemed to be missing from this experience.

We ruined our friendship, but I didn't expect her to chase after his dick a week later. After avoiding me so professionally it felt like a betrayal. So expertly I had to use location services when she wasn't at home watching movies the way she always did.

Instead, she was right here, fucking my carbon copy only a lot more enthusiastically.

Twisting around I forced myself to stop watching before I started to compare every move and every difference. The anger was a searing kind of hot that worked its way through my veins until it felt like the only thing I needed to survive.

I offered her the whole, I protected her, I loved her, and she still chose him.

My firsts were so tight I felt my hands go numb and my wrists hurt as I left them behind me. Pulling out my phone I saw the slew of texts from my father summoning me like his personal pet.

The anger seemed to simmer down when a wave of sadness hit in a heavy wave. Clover West didn't want me, and it felt like the end of the world. We shared a face and he still won. Her breathy moan wasn't my imagination at all - it was her truth.

None of the logic made it hurt any less.

In a fit of rage, I wanted to hurt them both so that was exactly what I did. There were only a few ways to do that. I had to relinquish my crown, forcing Ambrose to take my place. That alone would hurt Clover more than I ever could when he was forced to use her just to discard her later.

Finally, we'd be on the same page with our matching broken hearts.

# ACKNOWLEDGMENTS

*My fam: always and forever. Thank you for letting me be wild enough to chase my dreams.*

*Readers: You guys. Thank you so much for loving The Unholy Trinity as much as you do and giving me a break from Thatcher to dive headfirst into The Brotherhood. They demanded my attention and (dare I say it) I think Ambrose will blow Vane out of the water. We can all pick teams later though.*

*Dee-MF-Garcia: Black Widow designs = indescribable. You take the inside of my head and make it a reality. I cease to be underwhelmed. My jaw is still detached.*

*My editor: Z - always. I really was testing your ability to stick with me. I promise my ass is typing more and is distracted less.*

*Beta Readers: Danielle, Martha, Autumn, Amber and everyone who beta read this prequel. Your excitement was contagious and fueled me to the finish line of book one.*

# ABOUT THE AUTHOR

Alex King is a writer (mostly dark but who knows) who is better at writing villains you can't help but fall for. She's a Gemini with a Virgo son and Capricorn husband who strongly recognizes her enneagram 4 in every situation. Currently residing where white Jeeps reign and Dunkin is consumed more than water and there's lots of beautiful views.

Sign up for my mailing list to receive monthly updates, get exclusives, giveaways and all the details on my next book!

What to look forward to:

- Bad Heir (The Brotherhood of Bastards Book One)
- These Vindicated Savages (The Unholy Trinity Book Three)
- For the Love of Villains Anthology
- Twas the Night Anthology
- Sin for Me Anthology
- All Hollows Eve Anthology

Printed in Great Britain
by Amazon

37241117R00046